Obed has been a leader in education, influencing primary education schools to graduate medical education. He helped lead key national initiatives while helping imbed the values and behaviours that shift organizational behaviour. His experience includes establishing new schools, workshops, academic programs and minority-focused initiatives at an array of universities, and non-profits in New York City; including Touro College and the University of Medicine and Health Sciences. He holds a Bachelor's degree from SUNY Empire State College and a Master's degree from Stony Brook University. Obed's a regular columnist and his peer review research publications in diversity, management and sustainability can be found at *Medical Education Online, the Journal of Management and Sustainability and the Journal of International Research.*

Marcus Learns About the Different Types of Doctors

Obed Figueroa

AUSTIN MACAULEY PUBLISHERS™

LONDON * CAMBRIDGE * NEW YORK * SHARJAH

Copyright © Obed Figueroa (2020)

A CIP catalogue record for this title is available from the British Library.

ISBN 9781528909891 (Paperback)
ISBN 9781528959414 (ePub e-book)

www.austinmacauley.com

First Published (2020)
Austin Macauley Publishers Ltd
25 Canada Square
Canary Wharf
London
E14 5LQ

I dedicate this book to my family for their patience and personal sacrifice. In addition, I'd like to acknowledge all of the underrepresented and those not in medicine. Please know I was always listening and thinking about how to facilitate change.

A special thanks to all of the physicians who took the time to review and approve the content that applied to their speciality.

Why is there a need for this children's story book?

Why is this significant? In the field of medicine minority recruitment and enrollment continues to be a challenge for medical schools. Frequently identified as a contributor to this challenge, in part, is the lack of exposure to industry and/or mentorship to guide young people to study medicine. In the 2016–17 annual report from the Association of American Medical Colleges (AAMC), the data shows 53,042 applicants applying to medical school, out of which 21,030 matriculated into medical schools (AAMC, 2016). The report identifies that for men and women there is almost equal representation in the areas of enrollment where men represent 50.2% and women 49.8%. This is a good sign for gender equity; however, the same cannot be said for ethnic groups underrepresented in medicine (URMs). The annual AAMC report shows low medical school enrollments for African Americans at 7.1% and Hispanics at 6.3% as compared to Caucasians enrollment rates that are at 51.48% (AAMC, 2016). As a result, it is my intention with this children's story book to start the conversation as early as first and second grade. Our young people need to learn about their career options much earlier than high school.

The plot of this children's story book targets the grade level of elementary school age children. In particular, children that are from urban communities. The context of the story based in New York (Bronx) and its main characters are a grandmother and grandchild having several conversations as well as meeting healthcare professionals within their community. The grandchild expresses an interest in becoming a doctor

and the grandmother, being resourceful and a non-college graduate, uses a local community resource, their community health center. The grandmother realizes that at the health center she can expose her grandchild to relatable healthcare providers. The trip to the community health center provides them both with a rich, informative experience. The grandchild demonstrates reactions that range from excitement, confusion, enlightenment to a new way of viewing doctors' roles in healthcare. Both were able to meet a broad range of diverse practitioners and they both left the facility having learned more about healthcare career options.

Setting: New York City (Bronx). The characters in this story are a grandmother (Nanna/Mrs. Tyler) and grandchild (Marcus).

Marcus: (Looking towards his grandmother) "Nanna, I want to be a doctor when I grow up."

Nanna: "Marcus, you would be the first in our family. What made you think about that idea?"

Marcus: "I was just seeing the doctors on T.V. and I like how they help make people feel better."

Nanna: "You know, Marcus, there are different types of doctors. I know a place we can visit to learn more."

Marcus: "Really! Thanks Nanna."

Nanna: "Tomorrow, we will take a trip into town."

Nanna: "Marcus, this is our community health center. This is where people go when they want to see a doctor for help."

Marcus: "Can we go inside?"

Nanna: "Yes, we can. I called the manager and we can go inside and have a look around and meet some of the doctors."

Marcus: (Shows excitement) "Yahoo! The doctors will talk to us?"

Nanna: "Yes, doctors want people to take better care of themselves. They spend years in school learning how to help people in different kinds of ways."

Nanna: "Marcus, this is Tracy, she is the center's office manager. She helps the doctors by keeping their appointments organized."

Tracy: "Hi, Marcus, I hear that you want to become a doctor. If it's OK with you, I would like to introduce you to some of my friends here at the center."

Tracy: "Marcus, I would like to introduce you to Dr. Pena. She is a Dentist."

Dr. Pena: "Hi, Marcus, it's nice to meet you. I went to school for many years and learned how to help people that have problems with their teeth."

Marcus: Dr. Pena, I visit my dentist for checkups."

Dr. Pena: "Marcus, that's good to hear. I also do checkups for my patients."

Marcus: "Nanna, isn't that Dr. Nicholas over there?"

Nanna: "Where? Oh, I see her. Yes, Dr. Nicholas works here and she helped me when I had my foot pain. Let's go say hi."

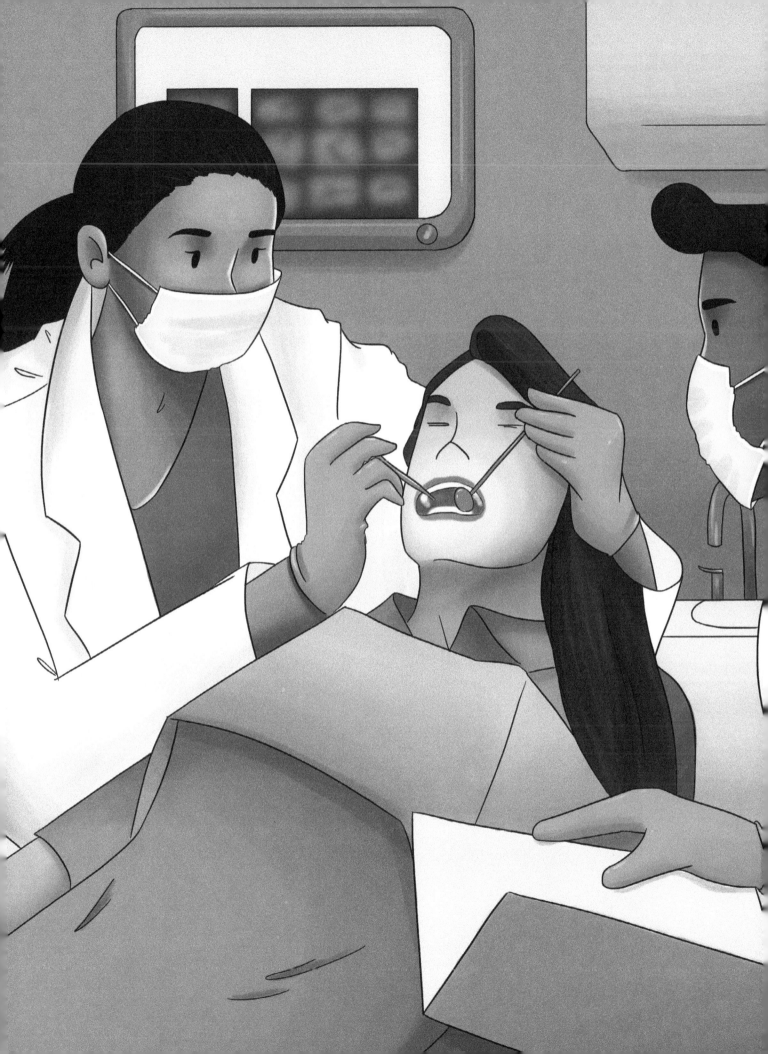

Marcus: "Hi, Dr. Nicholas!"

Dr. Nicholas: "Good to see you both. What brings you to the health center?"

Nanna: "Marcus wanted to meet some of your doctor friends."

Dr. Nicholas: "Marcus, I hear you are learning about the different kinds of doctors."

Marcus: "Yes, Dr. Nicholas, I did not know there were different kinds of doctors."

Dr. Nicholas: "Marcus, I am a Doctor of Podiatry. You usually see 'DPM' at the end of my name tag. I went to medical school and learned how to help people with foot pain. I can also do foot surgery if the patient needs that kind of help."

Marcus: "Dr. Nicholas, can you also help people with their teeth?"

Dr. Nicholas: "No, Marcus, I am only allowed to help people with things I learned in medical school. Dr. Pena went to school and she learned how to help people with problems they have with their teeth."

Nanna: "Thanks Dr. Nicholas for talking with us. Marcus, Tracy wants us to meet another doctor."

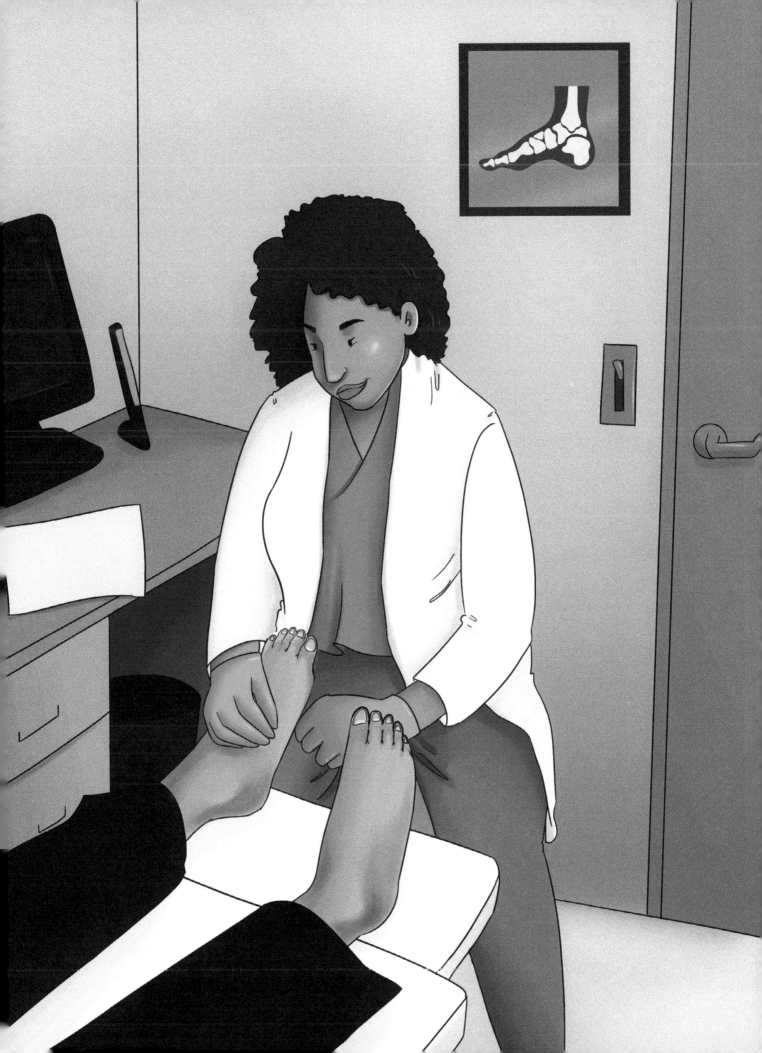

Tracy: "Dr. Blake, I would like you to meet Marcus and his grandmother, Mrs. Tyler."

Dr. Blake: "Good Morning to you both. I hear you are learning a lot about doctors today."

Marcus: "Yes, I am. Dr. Blake, what kind of a doctor are you?"

Dr. Blake: "Marcus, I am often called an internist or primary care doctor. I have MD after my name. This means 'medical doctor.' I went to medical school to learn how to help people figure out what's going on with their body. Sometimes I do checkups and sometimes I help people feel better when they're in pain."

Marcus: "Dr. Blake, I visit a doctor for checkups too. My school says that I have to get a yearly physical before I start school."

Dr. Blake: (He laughs) "Yes, Marcus, it was a rule for my school too. It's important that we take good care of our bodies."

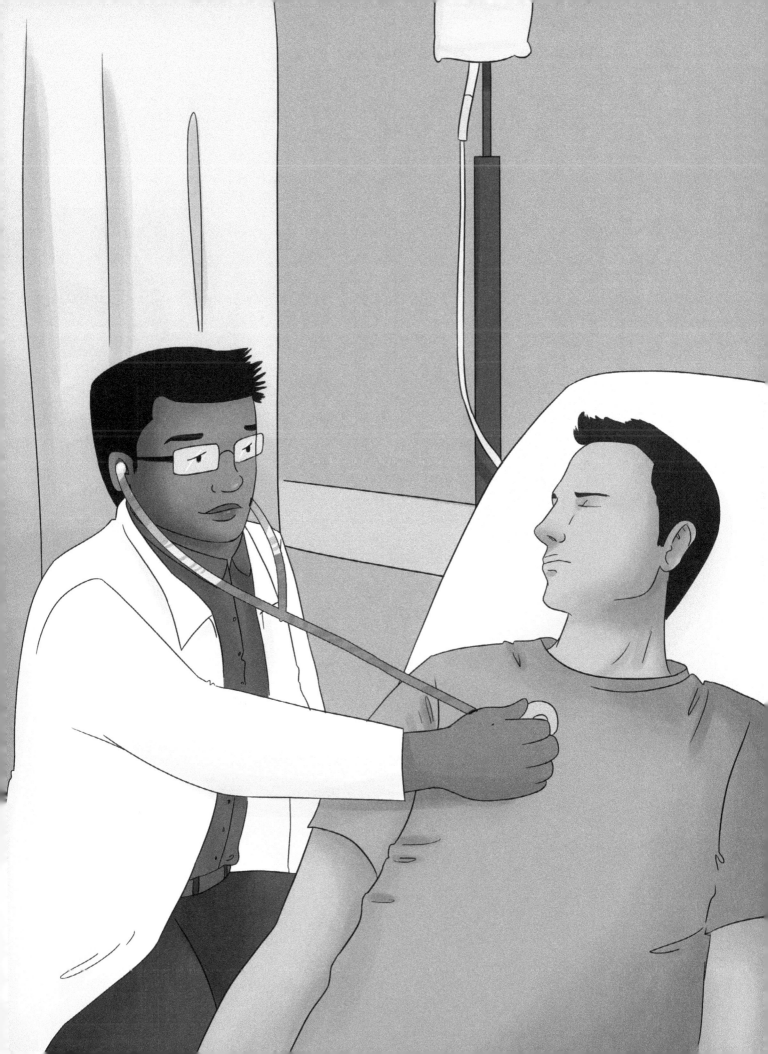

Tracy: "Mrs. Tyler, do you have time to meet some more of my friends at the center?"

Nanna: "Tracy, thank you. Marcus and I have to leave soon but we can meet a couple more of your doctors."

Tracy: "Great, Marcus, I would like you to meet Dr. Mesidor. She is a doctor of osteopathic (osteo-path-ek) medicine (DO)."

Marcus: "Dr. Mesidor, how does an osteo...path...thick doctor help people?"

Dr. Mesidor: "Marcus, I hear you've met some of my friends here. So Marcus, as Tracy mentioned, I am a doctor of osteopathic medicine. Do you see the D.O after my name?"

Marcus: "Yes, I was going to ask you what those letters meant."

Dr. Mesidor: "Marcus, I went to medical school and I learned how to help people figure out what is bothering their bodies by understanding the bones throughout our body. I learned about how things are connected in our body."

"Marcus, say you're feeling pain in your legs. Well it might be because your bones in your back may not be straight. I can help fix that problem which would make the pain go away."

Marcus: Wow! Dr. Mesidor, I did not know you could do that."

Tracy: "Thanks, Dr. Mesidor. Marcus, remember I told you that I was not a doctor but I help them."

Marcus: "Yes, I remember."

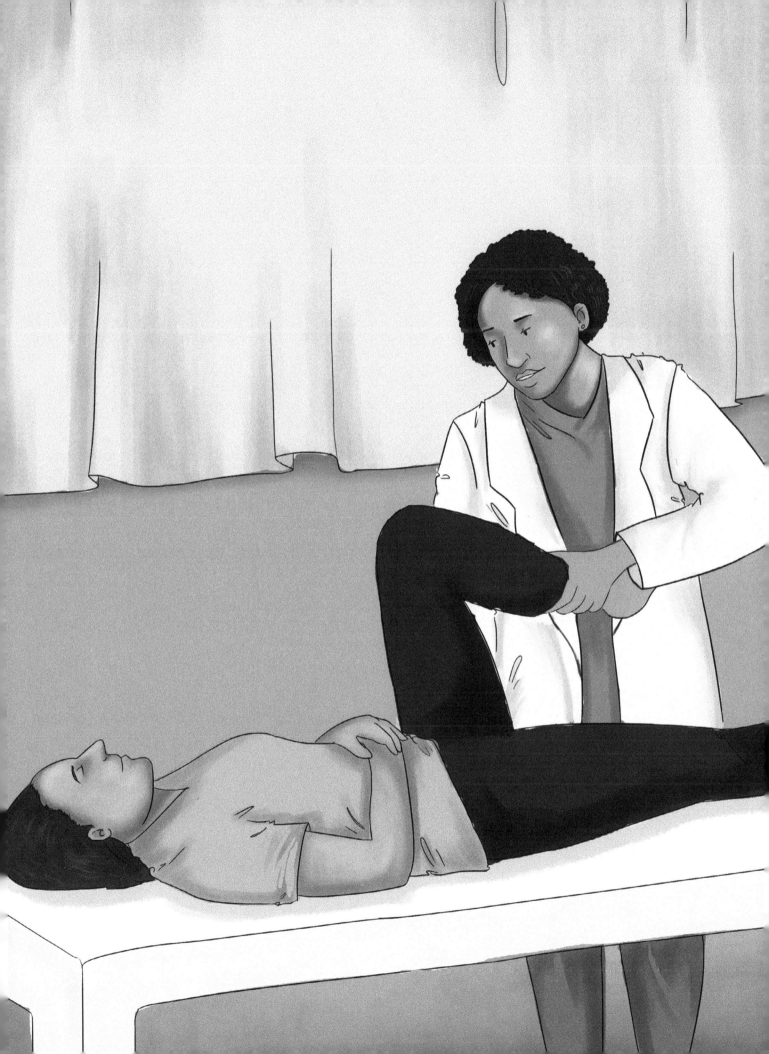

Tracy: Good, because I want you to also meet someone who also helps the doctors and patients. Marcus, meet Mr. Figueroa, he is a nurse."

Marcus: "Mr. Figueroa! I did not know boys can be nurses!"

Nurse Figueroa: "Marcus, (Laughing) you can call me Raymond and yes, boys are nurses too.
I went to school and learned a lot about our body and how to work with the doctors to help people. I meet patients and ask them important questions. I also give 'checkups' and if the doctor orders, I can also give the patient medication to make them feel better."

Marcus: "Raymond, you work with a lot of doctors and people. Do you ever get sad when someone comes to the center in pain?"

Nurse Figueroa: "Sometimes, but I have to remember that I went to school to help people in pain so I have to stay focused and work with my team to help the patients."

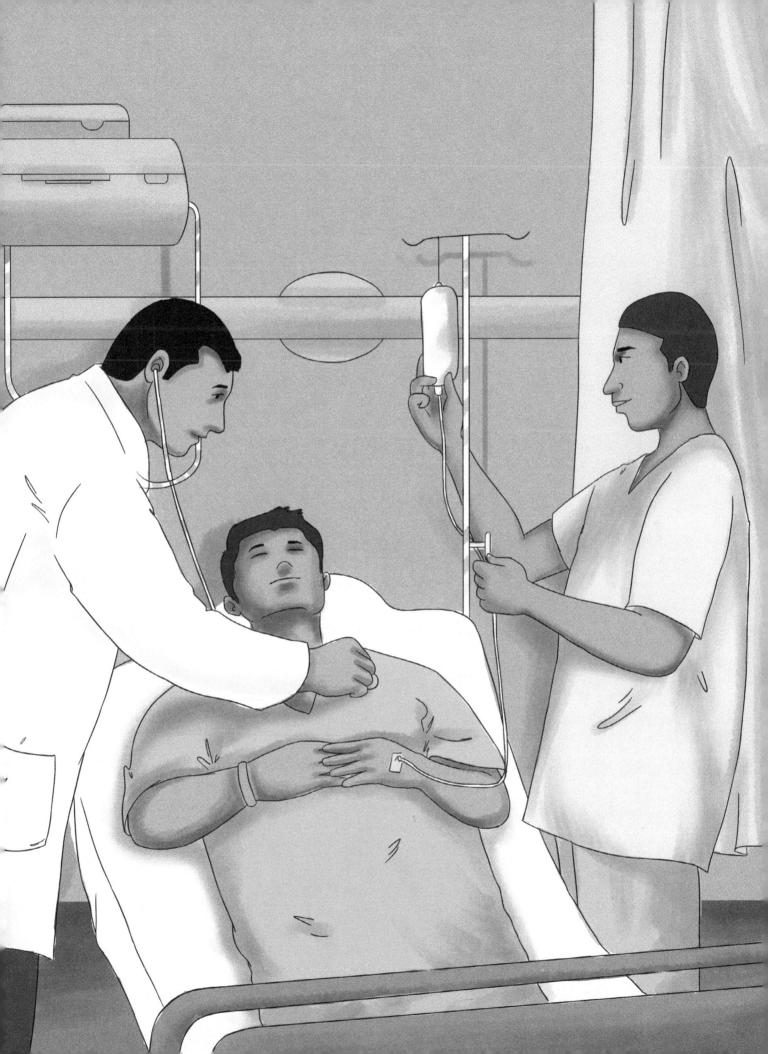

Nanna: "Tracy and Mr. Figueroa, thanks so much. Marcus and I appreciate everyone being so kind to answer our questions. We learned so much from our visit."

Tracy: "No problem Mrs. Tyler. I am glad we could help. Marcus, I look forward to calling you Dr. Marcus one day. Do well in school so you can learn all you need to help our community."

Marcus: "Mrs. Tracy, I will, and please tell the doctors I said it was nice to meet them."

Printed in the USA
CPSIA information can be obtained
at www.ICGtesting.com
CBHW082111100224
4219CB00060B/1921